My Snowman, Paul

Written by Yossi Lapid
Illustrated by Joanna Pasek

ISBN 978-0-9973899-0-6

I dedicate this book series to my beloved wife, Susan. Without your constant love and support, this book series would not have been possible.

It was a snowy winter day

And I was in a mood to play.

So mother said, "Hey listen, Dan.
Go build yourself a nice snowman."

"I don't know Mom, it's getting late,
And snowmen aren't all that great.
In fact, Bill says they're really dumb..."

"Well, that's his problem!" answered Mom.

"All right," I said, "so let me try..."

And, soon, my snowman stood up high.
'Cause it was awesome, I must say,
How well the snow packed on that day.

I had great fun for quite a while...

But then I saw Bill's mocking smile...

I thought I'd go in for a snack...
But then this voice snapped, "Hey,

How dare you think of jam and bread
When I'm still waiting for my head?"

I was amazed by what I heard,
I couldn't say another word,
I patched together head and all
And he said, "Hi!

My name is Paul!"

So I said, "Hi, my name is Dan...
Now, what's this all about, Snowman?"

"Well," answered Paul, "I'm here to play!"

"Too bad," I said. "You cannot stay!
Bill, over there, is watching us..."

"I see," said Paul. "But what's the fuss?
We simply want to have some fun!
How can that bother anyone?
No, I don't care about this Bill...

C'mon, I'll race you up that hill!"

And, then, we raced and hugged and all
And, now, my new best friend is Paul.

CPSIA information can be obtained
at www.ICGtesting.com
Printed in the USA
LVHW071907081220
672149LV00069B/480